WAGGERS

For Rainer, who is a dog's best friend.

WAGGERS

Written by **Stacy Nyikos**

Illustrated by **Tamara Anegón**

Sky Pony Press
New York

FREE PUPPIES
RAZORTAIL WHIPPETS

Waggers tried to be good. He tried really hard. When he saw Moni and Michael, he sat very straight and perked his ears. But when they picked Waggers up, his tail twirled so hard it sent the other puppies flying.

"That's some tail," said Mom.

"I'll say," said Dad.

"Yeah!" said Moni and Michael.
They begged and pleaded until Mom
and Dad were swayed. It was only a tail.
How much harm could it do?

They adopted Waggers and took him home.

"Let's make cookies," Moni said.
Waggers helped Moni get the
ingredients. He kept her company while
she mixed them up. He even tested the
dough without Moni having to ask.
Yum!
His tail started to wag.

Swoop! Swoop! Swoop! Swoop! **SWOOP!** Swoop!

"Waggers, no!" Moni said.
But it was REALLY good cookie dough.

"Bad dog, Waggers!" said Mom.

Waggers hung his head. He tried to be good. He tried really hard. But his tail got in the way.

"There's a monster," Michael whispered.
He crouched down. Waggers crouched
down. Michael crept toward the sofa.
Waggers crept, too. He even pounced
on the monster's shoes without Michael
having to ask.

Mmmmm!

His tail started to wag.

Whoop! Whoop! Whoop! Whoop! Whoop! **Whoop!**

"Waggers, no!" Michael said.
But they were REALLY stinky shoes.

"Bad dog, Waggers!" said Dad.
Waggers hung his head. He tried to be good. He
tried really hard. But his tail got in the way.

The next week,
Waggers practiced "sit."

The week after that, he
found hidden treasure.

And the week after that, Waggers stopped an alien invasion.

"Something's got to be done about that dog," said Mom.
"He's ruining our house," said Dad.

So Moni and Michael hid
Waggers in the garage.
   "Be good, Waggers," they said.
Waggers tried to be good. He
tried really hard.

But there was a fly in the garage—a REALLY loud fly.

Mom and Dad decided Waggers
needed a new home. Moni and
Michael begged and pleaded, but it
was no use. The house was falling
apart. It couldn't take one more wag.

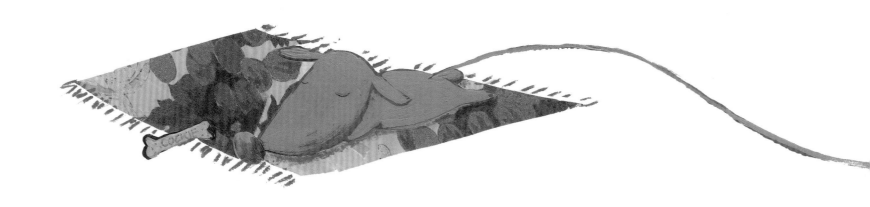

Moni, Michael, and Waggers spent their last night together in the backyard. They played and told stories and counted stars until Moni and Michael fell asleep. Waggers tried to sleep too, but he had an itch.

It was a REALLY bad itch. His tail started to twirl.

Waggers got up. He scratched. He rubbed. He wriggled all the way across the yard and back again. And again.

And again.
And again.
And again.

Ahhhh!

Waggers curled up next to Moni and Michael and fell asleep. He was so worn out his tail barely twitched. But oh, what it had done.

"My bushes!" said Mom.
"My yard!" said Dad.
Waggers tried to be good. He tried really hard. But his tail . . .

. . . his tail had cut the grass, trimmed the bushes, and even pruned the drooping branches.

"That's some tail," said Mom.

"I'll say," said Dad.

"Yeah!" said Moni and Michael.

It turned out Waggers didn't need a new home. He needed a new yard. Lots of them. Waggers swept leaves, piled snow, even painted fences.

By dinner each night, his tail was all wagged out.

"Good boy, Waggers!"

Waggers didn't have to try to be good anymore. He was good. He was the best dog ever, and his tail never got in the way again.

Well, almost . . .

Sky Pony Press books may be purchased in bulk at special discounts for sales promotion, corporate gifts, fund-raising, or educational purposes. Special editions can also be created to specifications. For details, contact the Special Sales Department, Sky Pony Press, 307 West 36th Street, 11th Floor, New York, NY 10018 or info@skyhorsepublishing.com.

Sky Pony® is a registered trademark of Skyhorse Publishing, Inc.®, a Delaware corporation.

Visit our website at www.skyponypress.com.

10 9 8 7 6 5 4 3 2 1

Manufactured in China, July 2014
This product conforms to CPSIA 2008

Library of Congress Cataloging-in-Publication Data

Nyikos, Stacy Ann.
Waggers / written by Stacy Nyikos ; illustrated by Tamara Anegón.
pages cm
Summary: "When Waggers, a well-meaning but clumsy dog, is adopted, he tries to be good; he really does. But it isn't Waggers's fault that his tail goes crazy when he gets excited. How much harm can a tail do, anyway?"—Provided by publisher.
ISBN 978-1-62914-629-4 (hardback)
[1. Dogs—Fiction. 2. Tail—Fiction. 3. Pet adoption—Fiction.] I. Anegón, Tamara, illustrator. II. Title.
PZ7.N9946Wag 2014
[E]—dc23
2014021417

Cover design by Brian Peterson
Cover illustrations credit Tamara Anegón
Book design by Sara Kitchen

Ebook ISBN: 978-1-63220-231-4